For all the Leos of this world, and especially for my very own one – I.M.

For Ollie and Isla – C.N.

First American Edition 2021
Kane Miller, A Division of EDC Publishing

Text copyright © 2021 by Isabelle Marinov
Illustration copyright © 2021 by Chris Nixon
Design copyright © 2021 by Templar Books
First published in the UK in 2021 by Templar Books,
an imprint of Bonnier Books UK,
The Plaza, 535 King's Road, London, SW10 0SZ.
Owned by Bonnier Books Sveavägen 56, Stockholm, Sweden.
Autism consultant: Professor Tony Attwood
Octopus consultant: Sarah Giltz, PhD

For information contact:
Kane Miller, A Division of EDC Publishing
5402 S 122nd E Ave, Tulsa, OK 74146
www.kanemiller.com
www.usbornebooksandmore.com

Library of Congress Control Number: 2020949020

Printed and bound in China
1 3 5 7 9 10 8 6 4 2

ISBN: 978-1-68464-277-9

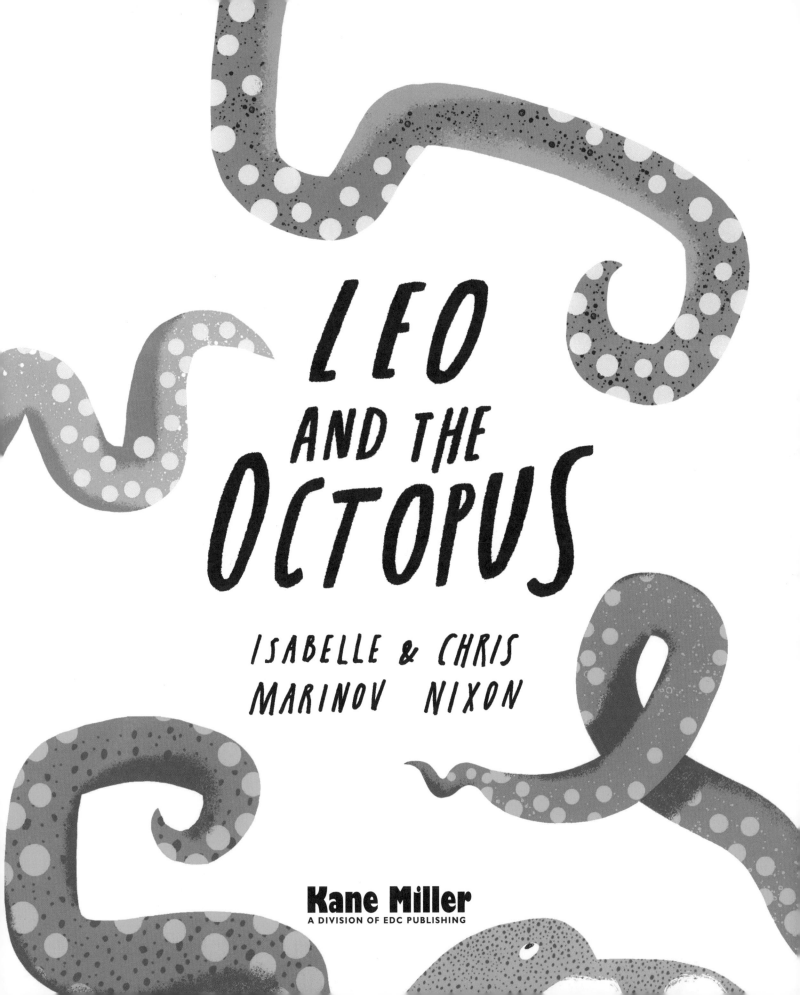

LEO
AND THE
OCTOPUS

ISABELLE & CHRIS
MARINOV   NIXON

Kane Miller
A DIVISION OF EDC PUBLISHING

The world was too bright for Leo. And too loud.
"I must be living on the wrong planet," he thought.

None of the other children understood Leo.
And he didn't understand them.

At home, Leo would hide inside his cardboard box to read.

Then he could **relax**.

Because life on the **wrong planet** was stressful.
And **tiring.**
And **lonely.**

Until the day Leo met Maya.

Maya was an octopus.

"She has eight arms, three hearts, and a beak like a parrot," said Edgar, the octopus keeper.

"She looks like an **alien**," Leo thought. "I *feel* like an alien. **We should get along.**"

Leo knew everything there was to know about lots of things.
But he didn't know anything about **octopuses** yet.
So he went to the library.

NOTES

OCTOPUSES HAVE BEEN AROUND FOR A LONG, LONG TIME — LONG BEFORE THE DINOSAURS! THEIR DISTANT RELATIVES ARE SNAILS.

THEY CAN CAMOUFLAGE THEMSELVES OR EXPRESS HOW THEY'RE FEELING BY CHANGING THEIR COLOR AND TEXTURE.

THEY RELEASE A CLOUD OF BLACK INK WHEN THEY ARE UNDER ATTACK TO CONFUSE THEIR PREDATORS.

OCTOPUSES CAN SOLVE PUZZLES AND OPEN CHILDPROOF JARS.

WITH THEIR SOFT, BONELESS BODIES, THEY CAN SQUEEZE INTO TINY CRACKS.

"Maybe Maya and I could become friends," Leo thought as he read. He didn't know much about friendship, but he was determined to give it a try.

The week after, Leo went
back to the aquarium to see Maya.
He told Edgar the octopus keeper
everything he had learned
about octopuses.

SO OLD!

NO BONES!

PUZZLE MASTERS!

Edgar was impressed. So impressed that he had an **idea.**
"Would you like to meet Maya?" he asked.
"You can touch her if you like."

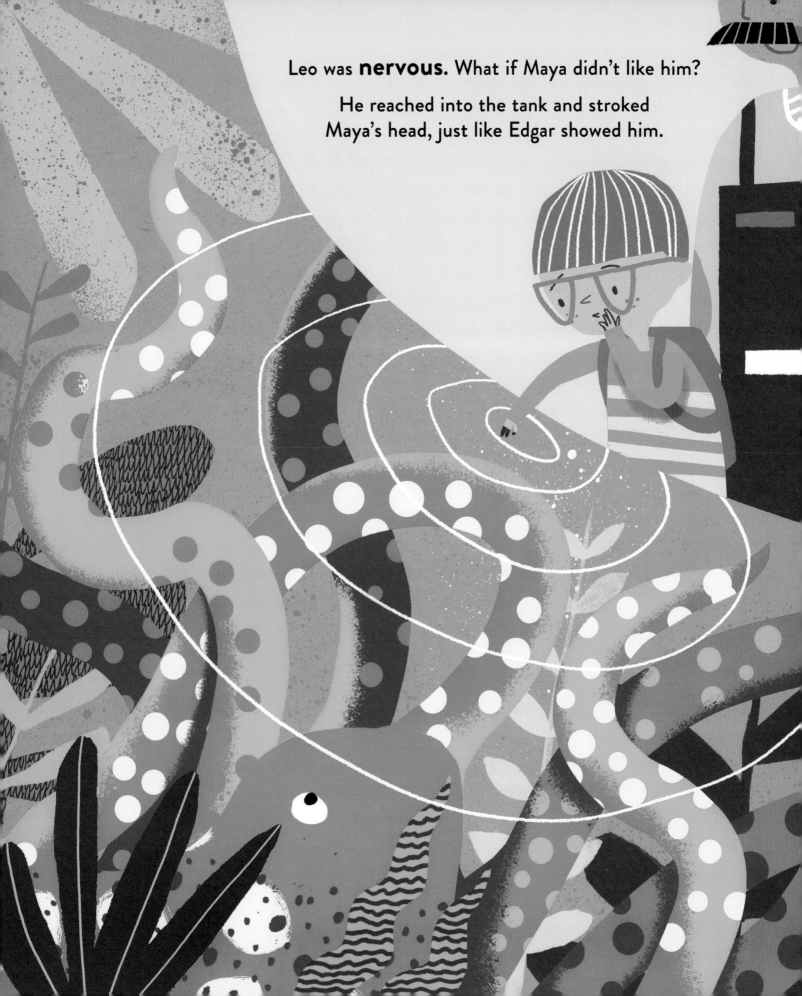

Leo was **nervous.** What if Maya didn't like him?

He reached into the tank and stroked Maya's head, just like Edgar showed him.

Leo was scared Maya would swim away, but she slowly reached out one arm.
As she touched Leo's hand, her skin started turning white and smooth.

Leo knew this was a **good sign.** It meant that Maya was feeling calm.
If only humans were as easy to understand!

"I think she likes you," said Edgar.
"Why don't you come back and visit every Friday?"
Leo was **excited.** From now on, Friday would be Octopus Day!

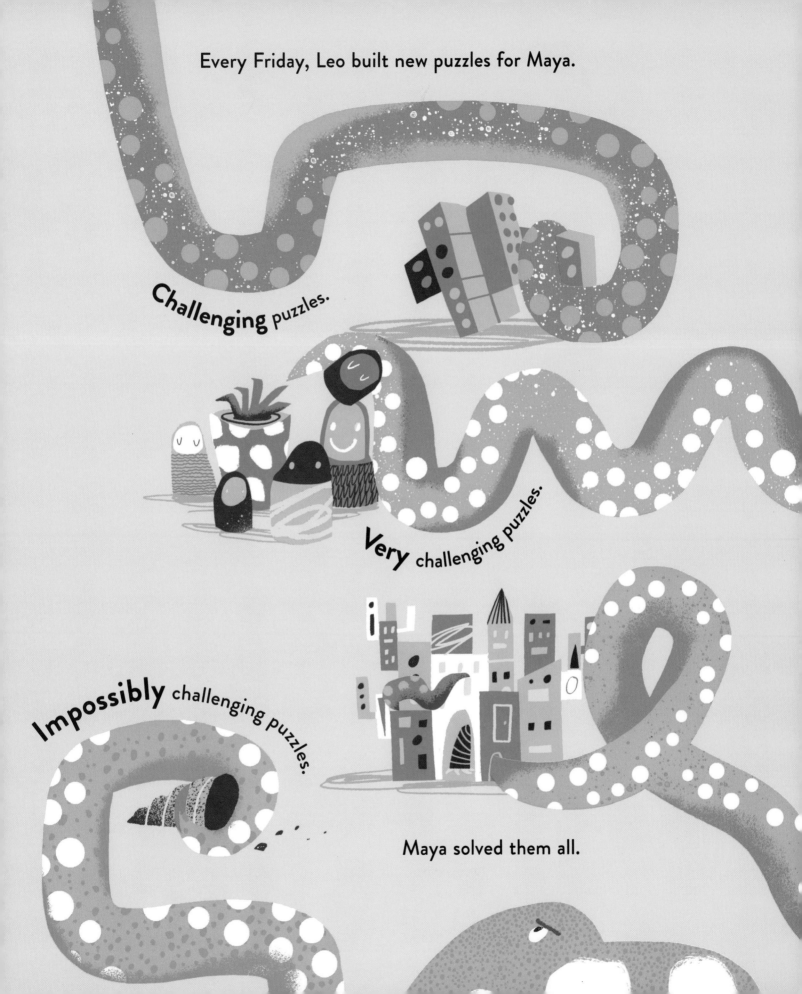

Every Friday, Leo built new puzzles for Maya.

Challenging puzzles.

Very challenging puzzles.

Impossibly challenging puzzles.

Maya solved them all.

One Friday afternoon,
when Leo arrived at the aquarium,
a lot of people had come to visit Maya.
Too many people.

"Maya doesn't like camera flashes,"
Leo thought. "Just like me."

Maya had turned red.
Leo knew this was a **bad sign.**
It meant that Maya was feeling **stressed.**

"**Watch out!**" Leo said.
But it was too late. In a split second,
Maya had darted to the surface
of the water . . .

. . . and hosed her visitors with a jet of cold water.

Leo knew exactly how Maya felt. Sometimes he wished he could squirt
water at all the things that annoyed him to make them disappear.

Leo wondered if Maya could use a pair of sunglasses.
But they probably wouldn't fit her, so he put up a sign instead.

Everyone had left – except for one small boy.

"Maya has eight arms, three hearts, and a beak like a parrot.
Would you like to meet her?" Leo asked.
After all, who wouldn't want to meet an **alien?**

The boy said: "Yes."

Maya touched the boy's arm.
Her skin turned smooth and white.
Leo knew this was a **good sign**.

"That means Maya likes you," he explained.

Then Leo told the boy all about **cute octopuses** shaped like umbrellas and **clever octopuses** pretending to be corals . . .

. . . and about **blanket octopuses** that look like superheroes and **argonaut octopuses** floating in shells . . .

The boy listened closely until Leo had told him everything he knew.

Then they walked home together.

Leo knew a little bit more about friendship now.
And he knew that this was a **good sign** too.

ISABELLE MARINOV

I've always been fascinated by octopuses, these strange, alien-like creatures.

When I learned that the giant Pacific octopus changes its color according to its mood, I was mesmerized. How convenient would this be for kids with autism! From my experience with my own son, I've seen that they often struggle to make sense of facial expressions in others. As visual learners, children on the spectrum would most certainly welcome this color-code communication. This simple idea was the seed for LEO AND THE OCTOPUS.

I am grateful to Tony Attwood for reviewing this story. His compassionate and pragmatic book *The Complete Guide to Asperger's Syndrome* is my reference whenever I struggle to understand my son's way of functioning.

PROFESSOR TONY ATTWOOD

This enchanting story describes the world as perceived by a child with autism and an octopus.

In some ways they both seem like aliens, and both share a talent for problem solving. As a child with autism, Leo finds it difficult to determine how someone is feeling by reading their facial expressions and body language. He appreciates how octopuses change color according to their mood and wishes humans had the same simple color code.

The story also illustrates another aspect of autism, that is, finding friendship through similar interests. The sensitive descriptions throughout the book of what it is like to have autism are accurate and perceptive on so many levels.